the

phone

goes

DEAD

For A. R. Claud -

something to get your teeth into

ORCHARD BOOKS
338 Euston Road,
London NW1 3BH
Hachette Children's Books
Orchard Books Australia
Level 17/207 Kent Street, Sydney, NSW 2000
First published in Great Britain in two volumes as
Horowitz Horror in 1999 and *More Horowitz Horror* in 2000
This edition published in 2002
Text © Anthony Horowitz 1999
The right of Anthony Horowitz to be identified as the author
of this work has been asserted by him in accordance with
the Copyright, Designs and Patents Act, 1988.
A CIP catalogue record for this book is available from
the British Library.
5 7 9 10 8 6
ISBN 978 1 84121 364 4
Printed in Great Britain

the
  phone
goes

DEAD

ANTHONY HOROWITZ

ORCHARD BOOKS

Contents

the

phone

goes

DEAD

This
is
how
Linda James
dies.

She's walking across Hyde Park in the middle of London when she notices that the weather has changed. The sky is an ugly colour. Not the blackness of nightfall but the heavy, pulsating mauve of an approaching storm. The clouds are boiling and seconds later there is a brilliant flash as a fork of lightning shimmers the entire length of the Thames.

It has been said that there are two things that you shouldn't do in a storm. The first is to make a telephone call. The second is to take shelter under a tree. Linda James does both of these things. As the rain begins to fall, she runs under the outstretched branches of a huge oak tree, then fishes in her handbag and takes out a mobile telephone.

She dials a number.

'Steve,' she says. 'I'm in Hyde Park.'

That's all she says. There's another flash of lightning

and this time Linda is hit full on. Seventy-five thousand volts of electricity zap through her, transmitted through the mobile phone into her brain. Her body jerks and the phone is thrown about twenty metres away from her. This is the last physical action Linda James ever makes and, it goes without saying, she is dead before the telephone even hits the ground.

We will never find out anything more about Linda. Was she married or single? Why was she crossing Hyde Park at six o'clock on a Wednesday evening and does it matter that, wherever she was going, she never arrived? Who was Steve? Did he ever find out that Linda was actually killed at the very moment she was speaking to him? None of these questions will ever be answered.

But the mobile phone. That's another story.

The phone is a Zodiac 555. Already old-fashioned. Manufactured somewhere in Eastern Europe. It is found in the long grass the day after the body has been removed and by a long, circuitous route, it ends up in a second-hand shop somewhere near the coast in the south of England. Despite everything, the phone seems to be working. Linda's SIM-card – the little piece of circuitry that makes it work – is removed. The phone is reprogrammed and another SIM-card put inside. Eventually, it goes back on sale.

And a few weeks later, a man called Mark Adams goes in and buys it. He wants a mobile telephone for his son.

David Adams holds the mobile telephone. 'Thanks, Dad,' he says. But he's not sure about it. A lot of his friends have got mobile phones, it's true. Half of them don't even make any calls. They just think it's cool, having their own phone – and the smaller and more expensive the model, the smarter they think they are. But the Zodiac 555 is clunky and out of date. It's grey. You can't snap on one of those multicoloured fronts. And Zodiac? It's not one of the trendier brand names. David has never heard of it.

And then there's the question of why his father has bought it in the first place. David is sixteen now and he's beginning to spend more time away from home, over-nighting with friends, parties on Saturday evening, surfing at first light on Sunday. He lives in Ventnor, a run-down seaside town on the Isle of Wight. He's lived his whole life on the island and maybe that's why he feels cramped, why he wants his own space. He's talking about sixth-form college and university on the mainland. Mark and Jane Adams run a hotel. They only have one son and they're afraid of losing him. They want to keep him near them, even when they can't see him. And that's why they've bought the mobile phone. David can imagine the next Saturday evening, when he's out with his mates at The Spyglass, the trill of Bach's Toccata and Fugue (which is what the phone plays when it rings) in his back pocket and his father or his mother checking up on him. 'You're only drinking lemonade, aren't you, David? You won't be home too late?'

But even so, it's his own phone. He can always turn it off. And now that he's started going out with Jill Hughes, who lives in the neighbouring village of Bonchurch and who goes to the same school as him, it could be useful.

Which is why he says, 'Thanks, Dad.'

'That's OK, David. But just remember. I'll pay the line rental for you, but the calls are down to you. It's ten pence a minute off-peak, so just be careful you don't talk too much.'

'Sure.'

They're a close family. For half the year there are just the three of them shuffling about in the twenty-three rooms of The Priory Hotel which stands on a hill, overlooking the beach at Ventnor. Mark and Jane Adams bought it ten years ago, when David was six. They got fed up with London and one day they just moved. Perhaps it was a mistake. The summer season on the Isle of Wight is a short one these days. Package holidays are so cheap that most families can afford to go to France or Spain where they're more sure of good weather. It gets busy around June but this is only March and the place is quiet. As usual it's hard to make ends meet. David helps his dad with the decorating and small maintenance jobs. Jane Adams has a part-time job with a yachting club in Cowes. The three of them get along. Mark still says he prefers Ventnor to London.

David isn't so sure. There are too many old people on the Isle of Wight. Everything feels run-down and neglected. People say that the whole place is fifty years behind the rest of England and he can believe it. Sometimes he looks at the waves, rolling into the shore, and he dreams of other countries – even other worlds – and wishes that his life could change.

It's about to.

The mobile phone rings at half past four one afternoon when David is on his way home from school. Bach's great organ piece reduced to a series of irritating electronic bleeps. Only about six people have his number. Jill, of course. His parents. A few other friends at school. But when David manages to find the phone in his backpack, dig it out and press the button, it is none of them on the line.

'Hello?' It's an old man.

'Yes?' David is sure that it's a wrong number.

'I want you to do something for me.' The old man

has one of those slightly quavering, do-what-you're-told voices. 'I want you to go and see my wife at Number Seventeen, Primrose Hill.'

'I'm sorry...' David begins.

'I want you to tell her that the ring is under the fridge. She'll understand.'

'Who is this speaking?' David asks.

'This is Eric. You know my wife. Mary Saunders. She lives at Number Seventeen and I want you to tell her...'

'I know,' David interrupts. 'Why can't you tell her?'

'I can't reach her!' The old man sounds annoyed now. As if he's stating the obvious. 'Will you tell her it's under the fridge? It's under the fridge. She'll understand what you mean.'

'Well...'

'Thank you very much.'

The phone goes dead. David hasn't even asked how Eric Saunders got his telephone number or why he should have rung it to ask him (why him?) to do this favour. But the fact is that David does vaguely know Mary Saunders. Ventnor being the sort of place it is, everyone more or less knows everyone but there's more to it than that. Mary Saunders used to work at the hotel. She worked in the kitchen but she retired about a year ago to look after her husband who had cancer or something. David remembers her; a small, plump, busy woman with a loud laugh. Always cheerful – at least, until she heard the news about her husband's illness. She used to bake cakes and she'd always be there with a cup of tea and a slice of something when David got back from school. She was all right. And Primrose Hill is only a few minutes' walk from where David is now, from where he took the call.

It's strange, Eric calling him this way, but David decides that after all it's not too much to ask. He hasn't even stopped walking. His footsteps carry him to Primrose Hill.

Number Seventeen is part of a long terrace of almost identical houses, tall and narrow, standing shoulder to shoulder on a steeply rising lane. Ventnor Down looms over them and they have no sea view. In fact most of the houses have no view at all. Lace curtains have been pulled over the windows to stop people looking in. As if anyone would want to.

Feeling slightly foolish, David rings the bell. Even as he hears the chimes, he changes his mind and wishes he hadn't come, wonders why Eric Saunders chose him and why he even listened. But it's too late. The door opens and there is Mary Saunders – just as he remembers her and yet not quite the same. She is older and thinner. She looks defeated and somehow David knows that she doesn't laugh so much any more. Even so, she's pleased to see him.

'David!' she exclaims. It's taken a moment or two to remember who he is and she's puzzled that he's come. 'This is a nice surprise! How are you?'

'I'm fine, thanks, Mrs Saunders.'

There's an awkward pause. David is embarrassed. She has been caught off guard.

'Do you want to come in?' she asks at last.

'No. No, thanks. I was just passing on my way home from school.'

'How are your parents? How's the hotel?'

'They're fine. Everything's fine.' David decides to get this over with as quickly as possible. 'I just got a phone call,' he says. 'I was asked to give you a message.'

'Oh yes?'

'It was Eric. He said to tell you that the ring is under the fridge...'

But already Mary's face has changed. She's looking at David as if he's just spat in her face. 'What...?' she mutters.

'He said it was under the fridge and that you'd understand.'

'What are you talking about? Is this some sort of joke?'

'No. It was him...'

'How can you be so cruel? How can you...?' She blinks rapidly and David sees, with a sort of sick feeling, that she's about to cry. 'I don't know!' she mutters and then she slams the door. Just like that. Slams it in his face.

David stands on the doorstep, bewildered. But not for long. He should never have come here and now he's glad to go. One of the net curtains in the house next door twitches. A neighbour has heard the slamming door and looks out to see what is going on.

But there's nobody there. Just a boy in school uniform, hurrying down the hill…

That night, at dinner, David mentions – casually – that he saw Mary Saunders. He doesn't tell his parents about the phone call. He doesn't mention the door shutting in his face.

'Ah, Mary!' His mother was always fond of the cook. 'I haven't seen her for a while. Not since the funeral.'

'Who died?' David asks. But he remembers Mary's face when he spoke to her. He already knows.

'Her husband. You remember Eric,' she says to Mark.

'He did some work in the garden.' Mark remembers now.

'Yes. Very sad. He had lung cancer. It wasn't surprising really. He was smoking twenty a day.' David's mother turns to him. 'You saw her today? How was she?'

'She was fine…' David says and he can't stop himself blushing. Someone played a joke on him. A stupid, malicious joke. Who was it? Who had his number and knew about Eric Saunders? Who telephoned him and imitated the old man's voice? Could it have been Jonathan Channon? Jonathan is his best friend at school and he's always had a mischievous side. But David can still hear the old man's voice and knows that it *was* an old man. Not a boy pretending to be a man. He knows it wasn't a joke.

And a few days later, David meets Mary Saunders again. He's walking down the High Street and he's just reached the old pile that used to be the Rex Cinema and suddenly she's there in front of him. He'd avoid her if he could but it's too late.

'Hello, Mrs Saunders,' he says. He's ashamed. He can't keep it out of his voice.

But now she's looking at him very strangely. She seems to be struggling with herself. There are tears in her eyes again but this time she's not unhappy. She's fighting with all sorts of emotions and it takes her a few seconds to find her voice, to find the words to say 'You came to see me.'

'I'm sorry,' David stammers. 'I didn't know...'

She raises a hand, trying to explain. 'My Eric died just

six weeks ago. It was a long illness. I nursed him to the end.'

'Yes. My mum told me. I didn't mean...'

'We both had wedding rings. We were married thirty-seven years ago and we each had a wedding ring. Just silver. Nothing very expensive. My ring was inscribed with his name. And his had mine, on the inside. And after he died, I looked for his ring, and I couldn't find it. It really upset me, that did. Because he'd never taken that ring off. Not once in thirty-seven years. And it was meant to be buried with him. That was what he'd always wanted.'

She stops. Takes out a tissue and dabs her eye.

'I don't know how you knew. What you told me... I don't want to know how you found out. But after you left me, I looked under the fridge. And the ring was there. He was so thin by the end, it must have fallen off his finger and rolled there. Anyway, David, I wanted you to know. I found the ring and the vicar's arranged for it to be put in the grave with my Eric. It means a lot to me. I'm glad you told me what you did. I'm glad...'

And she hurries on, up the hill. David watches her

go, knowing that she isn't angry with him any more. But now she's something else. She's scared.

That afternoon, the telephone rings again.

'You don't know me,' says the voice, and this time it's a woman, brisk, matter-of-fact. 'But I met someone and they gave me your number. They said you might be able to pass a message on.'

'Oh yes?' David can't keep the dread out of his voice.

'My name is Samantha Davies. I'd be very grateful if you could talk to my mother. Her name is Marion and she lives at Number Eleven, St Edward's Square, Newport. Could you let her know that I think it's quite wrong of her to blame Henry for what happened and that I'd be much happier if the two of them were talking again.'

Once again, the phone goes dead.

This time David doesn't just walk into it. This time, he makes enquiries. And he discovers that there is a Marion Davies who lives at Number Eleven, St Edward's Square in Newport which is the largest town in the Isle of Wight.

Mrs Davies is a retired piano teacher. Last year, her eldest daughter, Samantha, was killed in a car accident. Her boyfriend, Henry, was driving.

David doesn't pass on the message. He doesn't want to get involved with someone he has never met. Anyway, how could he possibly explain to Mrs Davies what he has heard on the phone?

The phone...

It begins to ring more often. With more and more messages.

'The name's Protheroe. Derek Protheroe. I got your number from Samantha Davies. I wonder if you could get in touch with my daughter in Portsmouth. She's seeing this young chap and he's lying to her. He's a crook. I'm very worried about her. Could you tell her her father says...'

'It's my mum. She's missing me so much. I just want her to know that I'm not in pain any more. I'm happy. I just wish that she could forget about me and get on with her life...'

'Do you think you could tell my wife that the bloody

solicitor's made a hash of the whole thing. I added a codicil to the will. I don't suppose you know what that means but she'll understand. It's very important because...'

'Miss FitzGerald. She lives in Eastbourne. This is her sister...'

On and on. After a few weeks, the phone is ringing six or seven times a day. Brothers and sisters. Husbands and wives. Sons and daughters. All wanting to get in touch.

And David doesn't tell anyone.

He wants to tell Jill, walking home with her from school. But she'd freak out. She'd think he was crazy. And he's afraid of losing her, his first real love. He wants to tell Jonathan Channon, his best friend. But Jonathan would only laugh. He'd think it was all a huge joke even though it doesn't amuse David at all. And above all he wants to tell his parents. But they're so busy, struggling to get the hotel ready for the next season. They've got plumbing problems, wiring problems, staff problems and – as always – money problems. He doesn't want to burden them with this.

But he knows. He is in communication with the dead. For some reason that he cannot even begin to understand, the Zodiac 555 has a direct line to wherever it is that lies beyond the grave. Do mobile telephones have lines? It doesn't matter. The fact is that a tiny gate has somehow opened up between this world and the next. That gate is the mobile phone. And as word has got round, more and more of the dead have been queuing up to use it. To get their messages across.

'Tell my uncle...'

'Can you speak to my wife...?'

'They have to know...'

Bach's Toccata and Fugue. Every time David hears the sound, it sends a shiver through his entire body. He can't bear it any more. In the end he turns the telephone off and buries it at the bottom of a drawer in his bedroom, underneath his old socks. But even then he sometimes imagines he can still hear it.

Diddley-dah.

Diddley-dah-dah...

He has nightmares about it. He sees ghosts and

skeletons, decomposing corpses. They are queuing up outside his room. They want to talk to him. They wonder why he doesn't reply.

Mark and Jane Adams get worried about their son. They notice that he's not sleeping well. He comes down to breakfast with a pale face and rings around his eyes. One of his teachers has told them that his work at school has begun to slip. They're worried that he might have split up with Jill. Could he be into drugs? Like every parent, they're quick to think the worst without actually getting anywhere near the truth.

They take him out to dinner. A little restaurant on Smuggler's Cove where fresh crabs and lobsters are dragged out of the sea, over the sand and on to the table. A close evening. Just the three of them.

They don't ask him any direct questions. That's the last thing you do with a teenager. Instead, they gently probe, trying to find out what's on his mind. David doesn't tell them anything. But towards the end of the meal, when the atmosphere is a little more relaxed, Mark Adams suddenly says, 'What happened to that mobile telephone we gave you?'

David flinches. Neither of his parents notice.

'You haven't used it in a while,' Mark says.

'I don't really need it,' David says.

'I thought it would be useful.'

'Well, I see everyone anyway. I'm sorry. I don't much like using it.'

Mark smiles. He doesn't want to make a big deal out of it. 'It's a bit of a waste of money,' he says. 'I'm paying the monthly rental.'

'Where is the phone?' his mother asks. She wonders if he's lost it.

'In my bedroom.'

'Well, if you don't want it, I might as well cancel the rental.'

'Yeah. Sure.' David sounds relieved. And he is.

That evening he gives the telephone back to his father and sleeps well for the first time in a week. No Bach. No dreams. It's finally over.

One week later.

Mark Adams is sitting in his office. It's a cosy, cluttered room at the top of the hotel, tucked into the eaves. There's a small window. He can see the sea sparkling in the sunlight. Outside, an engineer is working on the telephone lines. The hotel has been cut off for two hours. Mark has spent the morning working on the accounts. There are bills from builders and decorators. The new microwave in the kitchen. As always, they've spent much more money than they've actually made. Not for the first time, Mark wonders if they might have to sell.

He glances down and notices the mobile phone sitting on a pile of papers. He flicks it on. The battery is fully charged. He makes a mental note to himself. He ought to cancel the line rental. That's a waste of money.

And then there's a movement at the door and suddenly Jane is there. She's run all the way upstairs and she pauses in the doorway, panting. She's a short woman, a little overweight. Her dark hair hangs over her eyes.

'What is it?' Mark asks. He's alarmed. When you've been married as long as he has you can sense when something is wrong. He senses it now.

'I saw it on the television,' Jane says.

'What?'

'David...'

David is away from home. There's a school skiing trip to France. He left this morning with Kate Evans, Jonathan Channon, everyone in his class. They flew to Lyons. A coach met them at the airport. It took them on the two-hour drive to the resort at Courcheval.

Or should have.

'There's been an accident,' Jane explains. She's close to tears. Not because she knows something. But because she doesn't. 'It was on the news. A coach full of schoolchildren. English schoolchildren. It was involved in a crash with a delivery van. It came off the road. They said there were a lot of fatalities.'

'Is it David's coach?'

'They didn't say.'

Mark struggles to make sense. 'There'll be a

hundred coaches at Lyons airport,' he says. 'It's the spring half-term, for Heaven's sake. There are schools all over the country sending kids to France.'

'But David arrived this morning. That's when it happened.'

'Have you rung the school?'

'I tried. The phones aren't working.'

Mark glances through the window, at the engineer working outside. Then he remembers the mobile telephone. 'We can use this,' he says.

He picks it up.

The phone rings in his hand.

Bach's Toccata and Fugue.

Mark is surprised. He fumbles for the button and presses it.

It's David.

'Hi, Dad,' he says. 'It's me.'

bath
NIGHT

She
didn't like
the bath
from
the
start.

Isabel was at home the Saturday they delivered it and wondered how the fat, metal beast was ever going to make it up one flight of stairs, around the corner and into the bathroom. The two scrawny workmen didn't seem to have much idea either. Thirty minutes, four gashed knuckles and a hundred swearwords later it seemed to be hopelessly wedged and it was only when Isabel's father lent a hand that they were able to free it. But then one of the stubby legs caught the wallpaper and tore it and that led to another argument right in front of the workmen, her mother and father blaming each other like they always did.

'I told you to measure it.'

'I did measure it.'

'Yes. But you said the legs came off.'

'No. That's what you said.'

It was so typical of her parents to buy that bath, Isabel thought. Anyone else would have been into the West End to one of the smart department stores. Pick something out of the showroom. Out with the credit card. Delivery and free installation in six weeks and thank you very much.

But Jeremy and Susan Martin weren't like that. Ever since they had bought their small, turn-of-the-century house in Muswell Hill, north London, they had devoted their holidays to getting it just right. And since they were both teachers – he at a public school, she in a local primary – their holidays were frequent and long.

And so, the dining-room table had come from an antique shop in Hungerford, the chairs that surrounded it from a house sale in Hove. The kitchen cupboards had been rescued from a skip in Macclesfield. And their double bed had been a rusting, tangled heap when they had found it in the barn of a French farmhouse outside Boulogne. So many weekends. So many hours spent searching, measuring, imagining, haggling and arguing.

That was the worst of it. As far as Isabel could see, her parents didn't seem to get any pleasure out of all these antiques. They argued constantly – in the shops, in the market-places, even at the auctions. Once her father had got so heated he had actually broken the Victorian chamber-pot they had been fighting about and of course he'd had to buy it anyway. It was in the hall now, glued back together again, the all-too-visible cracks an unpleasant image of their twelve year old marriage.

The bath was Victorian too. Isabel had been with her parents when they bought it – at an architectural salvage yard in west London. 'End of the last century,' the dealer had told them. 'A real beauty. It's still got its own taps...'

It certainly didn't look beautiful as it squatted there on the stripped-pine floor, surrounded by stops and washers and twisting lengths of pipe. It reminded Isabel of a pregnant cow, its great white belly hanging only inches off the ground. Its metal feet curved outwards, splayed, as if unable to bear the weight. And, of course, it had been decapitated.

There was a single round hole where the taps would be and beneath it an ugly yellow stain in the white enamel where the water had trickled down for perhaps a hundred years, on its way to the plug-hole below. Isabel glanced at the taps, lying next to the sink, a tangle of mottled brass that looked too big for the bath they were meant to sit on. There were two handles, marked Hot and Cold on faded ivory discs. Isabel imagined the water thundering in. It would need to. The bath was very deep.

But nobody used the bath that night. Jeremy had said he would be able to connect it up himself but in the end he had found it was beyond him. Nothing fitted. It would have to be soldered. Unfortunately he wouldn't be able to get a plumber until Monday and of course it would add another forty pounds to the bill and when he told Susan that led to another argument. They ate their dinner in front of the television that night, letting the shallow laughter of a sitcom cover the chill silence in the room.

And then it was nine o'clock. 'You'd better go to bed early, darling. School tomorrow,' Susan said.

'Yes, Mum.' Isabel was twelve but her mother sometimes treated her as if she were much younger. Maybe it came from teaching in a primary school. Although her father was a tutor at Highgate School, Isabel went to an ordinary state school and she was glad of it. They didn't allow girls at Highgate and she had always found the boys altogether too prim and proper. They were probably all gay too.

Isabel undressed and washed quickly – hands, face, neck, teeth, in that order. The face that gazed out at her from the gilded mirror above the sink wasn't an unattractive one, she thought, except for the annoying pimple on her nose...a punishment for the Mars Bar ice cream she'd eaten the day before. Long brown hair and blue eyes (her mother's), a thin face with narrow cheekbones and chin (her father's). She had been fat until she was nine but now she was getting herself in shape. She'd never be a supermodel. She was too fond of ice cream for that. But no fatty either, not like Belinda Price, her best friend at school, who was doomed to a life of hopeless diets and baggy clothes.

The shape of the bath, over her shoulder, caught her eye and she realised suddenly that from the moment she had come into the bathroom she had been trying to avoid looking at it. Why? She put her toothbrush down, turned round and examined it. She didn't like it. Her first impression had been right. It was so big and ugly with its dull enamel and dribbling stain over the plug-hole. And it seemed – it was a stupid thought but now it was there she couldn't make it go away – it seemed to be *waiting* for her. She half-smiled at her own foolishness. And then she noticed something else.

There was a small puddle of water in the bottom of the bath. As she moved her head, it caught the light and she saw it clearly. Isabel's first thought was to look up at the ceiling. There had to be a leak, somewhere upstairs, in the attic. How else could water have got into a bath whose taps were lying on their side next to the sink? But there was no leak. Isabel leaned forward and ran her third finger along the bottom of the bath. The water was warm.

'I must have splashed it in there myself,' she

thought. 'As I was washing my face...'

She flicked the light off and left the room, crossing the landing to her bedroom on the other side of her parents'. Somewhere in her mind she knew that it wasn't true, that she could never have splashed water from the sink into the bath. But it wasn't an important question. In fact it was ridiculous. She curled up in bed and closed her eyes.

But an hour later her thumb was still rubbing circles against her third finger and it was a long, long time before she slept.

'Bath night!' her father said when she got home from school the next day. He was in a good mood, smiling broadly as he shuffled together the ingredients for that night's dinner.

'So you got it plumbed in then?'

'Yes.' He looked up. 'It cost fifty pounds - don't tell your mother. The plumber was here for two hours.' He smiled and blinked several times and Isabel was reminded of something she had once been told by the brother of a friend who went to the school where he taught. At school, her father's nickname was Mouse. Why did boys have to be so cruel?

She reached out and squeezed his arm. 'That's great, Dad,' she said. 'I'll have a bath after dinner. What are you making?'

'Lasagne. Your mum's gone out to get some wine.'

It was a pleasant evening. Isabel had got a part in her school play – Lady Montague in *Romeo and Juliet*. Susan had found a ten-pound note in the pocket of a jacket she hadn't worn for years. Jeremy had been asked to take a party of boys to Paris at the end of term. Good news oiled the machinery of the family and for once everything turned smoothly. After dinner, Isabel did half-an-hour's homework then kissed her parents good night and went upstairs.

To the bathroom.

The bath was ready now. Installed. Permanent. The taps with the black Hot and Cold protruded over the rim with the curve of a vulture's neck. A silver plug on a heavy chain slanted into the plug-hole. Her father had polished the brasswork, giving it a new gleam. He had put the towels back on the rail and a green bath-mat on the floor. Everything back to normal. And yet the room, the towels, the bath-mat seemed to have shrunk. The bath was too big. And it was waiting for her. She still couldn't get the thought out of her mind.

'Isabel. Stop being silly…!'

What's the first sign of madness? Talking to yourself. And the second sign? Answering back. Isabel let out a great sigh of breath and went over to the bath. She leaned in and pushed the plug into the hole. Downstairs, she could hear the television; *World in Action*, one of her father's favourite programmes. She reached out and turned on the hot tap, the metal squeaking slightly under her hand. Without pausing, she gave the cold tap a quarter-turn. Now let's see if that plumber was worth his fifty quid.

For a moment, nothing happened. Then, deep down underneath the floor, something rumbled. There was a rattling in the pipe that grew louder and louder as it rose up but still no water. Then the tap coughed, the cough of an old man, of a heavy smoker. A bubble of something like saliva appeared at its lips. It coughed again and spat it out. Isabel looked down in dismay.

Whatever had been spat into the bath was an ugly red, the colour of rust. The taps spluttered again and coughed out more of the thick, treacly stuff. It bounced off the bottom of the bath and splattered against the sides. Isabel was beginning to feel sick and before the taps could deliver a third load of – whatever it was – into the bath, she seized hold of them and locked them both shut. She could feel the pipes rattling beneath her hands but then it was done. The shuddering stopped. The rest of the liquid was swallowed back into the network of pipes.

But still it wasn't over. The bottom of the bath was coated with the liquid. It slid unwillingly towards the plug-hole which swallowed it greedily. Isabel looked more closely. Was she going mad or was there something *inside* the plughole? Isabel was sure she had put the plug in but now it was half-in and half-out of the hole and she could see below.

There was something. It was like a white ball, turning slowly, collapsing in on itself, glistening wet and alive.

And it was rising, making for the surface...

Isabel cried out. At the same time she leant over and jammed the plug back into the hole. Her hand touched the red liquid and she recoiled, feeling it, warm and clinging, against her skin.

And that was enough. She reeled back, yanked a towel off the rail and rubbed it against her hand so hard that it hurt. Then she threw open the bathroom door and ran downstairs.

Her parents were still watching television.

'What's the matter with you?' Jeremy asked.

Isabel explained what had happened, the words tumbling over each other in their hurry to get out, but it was as if her father wasn't listening. 'There's always a bit of rust with a new bath,' he went on. 'It's in the pipes. Run the water for a few minutes and it'll go.'

'It wasn't rust,' Isabel said.

'Maybe the boiler's playing up again,' Susan muttered.

'It's not the boiler.' Jeremy frowned. He had bought it second hand and it had always been a sore point – particularly when it broke down.

'It was horrible,' Isabel insisted. 'It was like...' What had it been like? Of course, she had known all along. 'Well, it was like blood. It was just like blood. And there was something else. Inside the plug.'

'Oh for heaven's sake!' Jeremy was irritated now, missing his programme.

'Come on! I'll come up with you...' Susan pushed a pile of Sunday newspapers off the sofa – she was still reading them even though this was Monday evening – and got to her feet.

'Where's the TV control?' Jeremy found it in the corner of his armchair and turned the volume up.

Isabel and her mother went upstairs, back into the bathroom. Isabel looked at the towel lying crumpled where she had left it. A white towel. She had wiped her hands on it. She was surprised to see there was no trace of a stain.

'What a lot of fuss over a teaspoon of rust!' Susan was leaning over the bath. Isabel stepped forward and peered in nervously. But it was true. There was a shallow puddle of water in the middle and a few grains of reddish rust. 'You know there's always a little rust in the system,' her mother went on. 'It's that stupid boiler of your father's.' She pulled out the plug. 'Nothing in there either!' Finally, she turned on the tap. Clean, ordinary water gushed out in a reassuring torrent. No rattling. No gurgles. Nothing. 'There you are. It's sorted itself out.'

Isabel hung back, leaning miserably against the sink. Her mother sighed. 'You were making it all up, weren't you?' she said – but her voice was affectionate, not angry.

'No, Mum.'

'It seems a long way to go to get out of having a bath.'

'I wasn't…!'

'Never mind now. Clean your teeth and go to bed.' Susan kissed her. 'Good night, dear. Sleep well.'

But that night Isabel didn't sleep at all.

She didn't have a bath the following night either. Jeremy Martin was out – there was a staff meeting at the school – and Susan was trying out a new Delia

Smith recipe for a dinner party the following weekend. She spent the whole evening in the kitchen.

Nor did Isabel have a bath on Wednesday. That was three days in a row and she was beginning to feel more than uncomfortable. She liked to be clean. That was her nature and as much as she tried flannelling herself using the sink, it wasn't the same. And it didn't help that her father had used the bath on Tuesday morning and her mother on Tuesday and Wednesday and neither of them had noticed anything wrong. It just made her feel more guilty – and dirtier.

Then on Thursday morning someone made a joke at school – something about rotten eggs – and as her cheeks burned, Isabel decided enough was enough. What was she so afraid of anyway? A sprinkling of rust which her imagination had turned into...something else. Susan Martin was out that evening – she was at her Italian evening class – so Isabel and her father sat down together to eat the Delia Smith crab cakes which hadn't quite worked because they had all fallen to pieces in the pan.

At nine o'clock they went their separate ways – he

to the News, she upstairs.

'Good night, Dad.'

'Good night, Is.'

It had been a nice, companionable evening.

And there was the bath, waiting for her. Yes. It *was* waiting, as if to receive her. But this time Isabel didn't hesitate. If she was as brisk and as businesslike as possible, she had decided, then nothing would happen. She simply wouldn't give her imagination time to play tricks on her. So without even thinking about it, she slipped the plug into the hole, turned on the taps and added a squirt of Body Shop avocado bubble bath for good measure. She undressed (her clothes were a useful mask, stopping her seeing the water as it filled) and only when she was quite naked did she turn round and look at the bath. It was fine. She could just see the water, pale green beneath a thick layer of foam. She stretched out her hand and felt the temperature. It was perfect: hot enough to steam up the mirror but not so hot as to scald. She turned off the taps. They dripped loudly as she remembered and went over to lock the door.

Yet still she hesitated. She was suddenly aware of her nakedness. It was as if she were in a room full of people. She shivered. 'You're being ridiculous,' she told herself. But the question hung in the air along with the steam from the water. It was like a nasty, unfunny riddle.

When are you at your most defenceless?

When you're naked, enclosed, lying on your back...

...in the bath.

'Ridiculous.' This time she actually said the word. And in one swift movement, a no-go-back decision, she got in.

The bath had tricked her – but she knew it too late.

The water was not hot. It wasn't even warm. She had tested the temperature moments before. She had seen the steam rising. But the water was colder than anything Isabel had ever felt. It was like breaking through the ice on a pond on a midwinter's day. As she sank helplessly into the bath, felt the water slide over her legs and stomach, close in on her throat like a clamp, her breath was punched back and her heart seemed to stop in mid-beat. The cold hurt her. It cut into her. Isabel opened her mouth and screamed as loudly as she could. The sound was nothing more than a choked-off whimper.

Isabel was being pulled under the water. Her neck hit the rim of the bath and slid down. Her long hair floated away from her. The foam slid over her mouth, then over her nose. She tried to move but her arms and legs wouldn't obey the signals she sent them. Her bones had frozen. The room seemed to be getting dark.

But then, with one final effort, Isabel twisted round and threw herself up, over the edge. Water exploded everywhere, splashing on to the floor. Then somehow she was lying down with foam all around her, sobbing and shivering, her skin completely white. She reached out and caught the corner of a towel, pulled it over her. Water trickled off her back and disappeared through the cracks in the floorboards.

Isabel lay like that for a long time. She had been scared…scared almost to death. But it wasn't just the change in the temperature of the water that had done it. It wasn't just the bath – as ugly and menacing as it was. No. It was the sound she had heard as she heaved herself out and jack-knifed on to the floor. She had heard it inches away from her ear, in the bathroom, even though she was alone.

Somebody had laughed.

'You don't believe me, do you?'

Isabel was standing at the bus-stop with Belinda Price; fat, reliable Belinda, always there when you needed her, her best friend. A week had passed and all the time it had built up inside her, what had happened in the bathroom, the story of the bath. But still Isabel had kept it to herself. Why? Because she was afraid of being laughed at? Because she was afraid no one would believe her? Because, simply, she was afraid. In that week she had done no work... at school or at home. She had been told off twice in class. Her clothes and her hair were in a state. Her eyes were dark with lack of sleep. But in the end she couldn't hold it back any more. She had told Belinda.

And now the other girl shrugged. 'I've heard of

haunted houses,' she muttered. 'And haunted castles. I've even heard of a haunted car. But a haunted bath...?'

'It happened, just like I said.'

'Maybe you think it happened. If you think something hard enough it can often...'

'It wasn't my imagination,' Isabel interrupted.

Then the bus came and the two girls got on, showing their passes to the driver. They took their seats on the top deck, near the back. They always sat in the same place without quite knowing why.

'You can't keep coming round to my place,' Belinda said. 'I'm sorry Bella, but my mum's beginning to ask what's going on.'

'I know.' Isabel sighed. She had managed to go round to Belinda's house three nights running and had showered there, grateful for the hot, rushing water. She had told her parents that she and Belinda were working on a project. But Belinda was right. It couldn't go on for ever.

The bus reached the traffic lights and turned on to the main road. Belinda screwed up her face, deep in thought. All the teachers said how clever she was, not just because she worked hard but because she let you see it. 'You say the bath is an old one,' she said at last.

'Yes?'

'Do you know where your parents got it?'

Isabel thought back. 'Yes. I wasn't with them when they bought it but it came from a place in Fulham. I've been there with them before.'

'Then why don't you go and ask them about it? I mean, if it is haunted there must be a reason. There's always a reason, isn't there?'

You mean...someone might have died in it or something? The thought made Isabel shiver.

'Yes. My gran had a heart attack in the bath. It didn't kill her though...'

'You're right!' The bus was climbing the hill now. Muswell Hill Broadway was straight ahead. Isabel gathered her things. 'I could go there on Saturday. Will you come too?'

'My mum and dad wouldn't let me.'

'You can tell them you're at my place. And I'll tell

my parents I'm at yours.'

'What if they check?'

'They never do.' The thought made Isabel sad. Her parents never did wonder where she was, never seemed to worry about her. They were too wrapped up in themselves.

'Well...I don't know...'

'Please, Belinda. On Saturday. I'll give you a call.'

That night the bath played its worst trick yet.

Isabel hadn't wanted to have a bath. During dinner she'd made a point of telling her parents how tired she was, how she was looking forward to an early night. But her parents were tired too. The atmosphere around the table had been distinctly jagged and Isabel found herself wondering just how much longer the family could stay together. Divorce. It was a horrible word, like an illness. Some of her friends had been off school for a week and then come back pale and miserable and had never been quite the same again. They'd caught it...divorce.

'Upstairs, young lady!' Her mother's voice broke into her thoughts. 'I think you'd better have a bath...'

'Not tonight, Mum.'

'Tonight. You've hardly used that bath since it was installed. What's the matter with you? Don't you like it?'

'No. I don't...'

That made her father twitch with annoyance. 'What's wrong with it?' he asked, sulking.

But before she could answer, her mother chipped in. 'It doesn't matter what's wrong with it. It's the only bath we've got so you're just going to have to get used to it.'

'I won't!'

Her parents looked at each other, momentarily helpless. Isabel realised that she had never defied them before – not like this. They were thrown. But then her mother stood up. 'Come on, Isabel,' she said. 'I've had enough of this stupidity. I'll come with you.'

And so the two of them went upstairs, Susan with that pinched, set look which meant she couldn't be argued with. But Isabel didn't argue with her. If her mother ran the bath, she would see for herself what was happening. She would see that something was wrong...

'Right...' Susan pushed the plug in and turned on the taps. Ordinary clear water gushed out. 'I really don't understand you, Isabel,' she exclaimed over the roar of the water. 'Maybe you've been staying up too late. I thought it was only six-year-olds who didn't like having baths. There!' The bath was full. Susan tested the water, swirling it round with the tips of her fingers. 'Not too hot. Now let's see you get in.'

'Mum...'

'You're not shy in front of me, are you? For heaven's sake...!'

Angry and humiliated, Isabel undressed in front of her mother, letting the clothes fall in a heap on the floor. Susan scooped them up but said nothing. Isabel hooked one leg over the edge of the bath and let her toes come into contact with the water. It was hot – but not scalding. Certainly not icy cold.

'Is it all right?' her mother asked.

'Yes, Mum...'

Isabel got into the bath. The water rose hungrily to

greet her. She could feel it close in a perfect circle around her neck. Her mother stood there a moment longer, holding her clothes. 'Can I leave you now?' she asked.

'Yes.' Isabel didn't want to be alone in the bathroom but she felt uncomfortable lying there with her mother hovering over her.

'Good.' Susan softened for a moment. 'I'll come and kiss you good night.' She held the clothes up and wrinkled her nose. 'These had better go in the wash too.'

Susan went.

Isabel lay there on her own in the hot water, trying to relax. But there was a knot in her stomach and her whole body was rigid, shying away from the cast-iron touch of the bath. She heard her mother going back down the stairs. The door of the laundry room opened. Isabel turned her head slightly and for the first time caught sight of herself in the mirror. And this time she did scream.

And screamed.

In the bath, everything was ordinary, just as it was when her mother had left her. Clear water. Her flesh a little pink in the heat. Steam. But in the mirror, in the reflection...

The bathroom was a slaughterhouse. The liquid in the bath was crimson and Isabel was up to her neck in it. As her hand – her reflected hand – recoiled out of the water, the red liquid clung to it, dripping down heavily, splattering against the side of the bath and clinging there too. Isabel tried to lever herself out of the bath but slipped and fell, the water rising over her chin. It touched her lips and she screamed again, certain she would be sucked into it and die. She tore her eyes away from the mirror. Now it was just water. In the mirror...

Blood.

She was covered in it, swimming in it. And there was somebody else in the room. Not in the room. In the reflection of the room. A man, tall, in his forties, dressed in some sort of suit, grey face, moustache, small, beady eyes.

'Go away!' Isabel yelled. 'Go away! Go away!'

When her mother found her, curled up on the floor in a huge puddle of water, naked and trembling, she didn't try to explain. She didn't even speak. She allowed herself to be half-carried into bed and hid herself, like a small child, under the duvet.

For the first time, Susan Martin was more worried than annoyed. That night, she sat down with Jeremy and the two of them were closer than they had been for a long time as they talked about their daughter, her behaviour, the need perhaps for some sort of therapy. But they didn't talk about the bath – and why should they? When Susan had burst into the bathroom she had seen nothing wrong with the water, nothing wrong with the mirror, nothing wrong with the bath.

No, they both agreed. There was something wrong with Isabel. It had nothing to do with the bath.

The antiques shop stood on the Fulham Road, a few minutes' walk from the tube station. From the front it looked like a grand house that might have belonged to a rich family perhaps a hundred years ago: tall imposing doors, shuttered windows, white stone columns and great chunks of statuary scattered on the pavement outside. But over the years the house had declined, the plaster-work falling away, weeds sprouting in the brickwork. The windows were dark with the dust of city life and car exhaust fumes.

Inside, the rooms were small and dark – each one filled with too much furniture. Isabel and Belinda passed through a room with fourteen fireplaces, another with half-a-dozen dinner tables and a crowd of empty chairs. If they hadn't known all these objects were for sale, they could have imagined that the place was still occupied by a rich madman. It was still more of a house than a shop. When the two girls spoke to each other, they did so in whispers.

They eventually found a sales assistant in a courtyard at the back of the house. This was a large, open area, filled with baths and basins, more statues, stone fountains, wrought-iron gates and trellis-work – all surrounded by a series of concrete arches that made them feel that they could have been in Rome or Venice rather than a shabby corner of west London. The assistant was a young man with a squint and a broken nose. He was carrying a gargoyle. Isabel wasn't sure which of the two were uglier.

'A Victorian bath?' he muttered in response to Isabel's enquiry. 'I don't think I can help you. We sell a lot of old baths.'

'It's big and white,' Isabel said. 'With little legs and gold taps...'

The sales assistant set the gargoyle down. It clunked heavily against a paving stone. 'Do you have the receipt?' he asked.

'No.'

'Well...what did you say your parents' name was?'

'Martin. Jeremy and Susan Martin.'

'Doesn't ring a bell...'

'They argue a lot. They probably argued about the price.'

A slow smile spread across the assistant's face. Because of the way his face twisted, the smile was oddly menacing. 'Yeah. I do remember,' he said. 'It was delivered somewhere in north London.'

'Muswell Hill,' Isabel said.

'That's right.' The smile cut its way over his cheekbones. 'I do remember. They got the Marlin bath.'

'What's the Marlin bath?' Belinda asked. She already didn't like the sound of it.

The sales assistant chuckled to himself. He pulled out a packet of ten cigarettes and lit one. It seemed a long time before he spoke again. 'Jacob Marlin. It was his bath. I don't suppose you've ever heard of him.'

'No,' Isabel said, wishing he'd get to the point.

'He was famous in his time.' The assistant blew silvery grey smoke into the air. 'Before they hanged him.'

'Why did they hang him?' Isabel asked.

'For murder. He was one of those…what do you call them…Victorian axe-murderers. Oh yes…' The sales assistant was grinning from ear to ear now, enjoying himself. 'He used to take young ladies home with him – a bit like Jack the Ripper. Know what I mean? Marlin would do away with them…'

'You mean kill them?' Belinda whispered.

'That's exactly what I mean. He'd kill them and then chop them up with an axe. In the bath.' The assistant sucked at his cigarette. 'I'm not saying he did it in that bath, mind. But it came out of his house. That's why it was so cheap. I dare say it would have been cheaper still if your mum and dad had known...'

Isabel turned and walked out of the antiques shop. Belinda followed her. Suddenly the place seemed horrible and menacing, as if every object on display might have some dreadful story attached to it. Only in the street, surrounded by the noise and colour of the traffic, did they stop and speak.

'It's horrible!' Belinda gasped. 'He cut people up in the bath and you...' She couldn't finish the sentence.

'I wish I hadn't come.' Isabel was close to tears. 'I wish they'd never bought the rotten thing.'

'If you tell them...'

'They won't listen to me. They never listen to me.'

'So what are you going to do?' Belinda asked.

Isabel thought for a moment. People pushed past on the pavement. Market vendors shouted their wares. A pair of policemen stopped briefly to examine some apples. It was a different world to the one they had left behind in the antiques shop. 'I'm going to destroy it,' she said at last. 'It's the only way. I'm going to break it up. And my parents can do whatever they like…'

She chose a monkey-wrench from her father's tool-box. It was big and she could use it both to smash and to unscrew. Neither of her parents were at home. They thought she was over at Belinda's. That was good. By the time they got back it would all be over.

There was something very comforting about the tool, the coldness of the steel against her palm, the way it weighed so heavily in her hand. Slowly she climbed the stairs, already imagining what she had to do. Would the monkey-wrench be strong enough to crack the bath? Or would she only disfigure it so badly that her parents would have to get rid of it? It didn't matter either way. She was doing the right thing. That was all she cared about.

The bathroom door was open. She was sure it had been shut when she had glanced upstairs only minutes before. But that didn't matter either. Swinging the monkey-wrench, she went into the bathroom.

The bath was ready for her.

It had filled itself to the very brim with hot water – scalding hot judging from the amount of steam. The mirror was completely misted over. A cool breeze from the door touched the surface of the glass and water trickled down. Isabel lifted the monkey-wrench. She was smiling a little cruelly. The one thing the bath couldn't do was move. It could taunt her and frighten her but now it just had to sit there and take what was coming to it.

She reached out with the monkey-wrench and jerked out the plug.

But the water didn't leave the bath. Instead, something thick and red oozed out of the plug-hole and floated up through the water.

Blood.

And with the blood came maggots – hundreds of them, uncoiling themselves from the plug-hole, forcing themselves up through the grille and cart-wheeling crazily in the water. Isabel stared in horror, then raised the monkey-wrench. The water, with the blood added to it, was sheeting over the side now, cascading on to the floor. She swung and felt her whole body shake as the metal clanged into the taps, smashing the C of Cold and jolting the pipe-work.

She lifted the monkey-wrench and as she did so she caught sight of it in the mirror. The reflection was blurred by the coating of steam but behind it she could make out another shape which she knew she would not see in the bathroom. A man was walking towards her as if down a long corridor, making for the glass that covered its end.

Jacob Marlin.

She felt his eyes burning into her and wondered what he would do when he reached the mirror that seemed to be a barrier between his world and hers.

She swung with the monkey-wrench – again and again. The tap bent, then broke off with the second impact. Water spurted out as if in a death-throe. Now she turned her attention to the bath itself, bringing the monkey-wrench crashing into the side, cracking the enamel with one swing, denting the metal with the next. Another glance over her shoulder told her that Marlin was getting closer, pushing his way towards the steam. She could see his teeth, discoloured and sharp, his gums exposed as his lips were drawn back in a grin of pure hatred. She swung again and saw – to her disbelief – that she had actually cracked the side of the bath like an eggshell. Red water gushed over her legs and feet. Maggots were sent spinning in a crazy dance across the bathroom floor, sliding into the cracks and wriggling there, helpless. How close was Marlin? Could he pass through the mirror? She lifted the monkey-wrench one last time and screamed as a pair of man's hands fell on her shoulders. The monkey-wrench span out of her hands and fell into the bath, disappearing in the murky water. The hands were at her throat now, pulling her backwards. Isabel screamed and lashed out, her nails going for the man's eyes.

She only just had time to realise that it was not Marlin who was holding her but her father. That her mother was standing in the doorway, staring with wide, horror-filled eyes. Isabel felt all the strength rush out of her body like the water out of the bath. The water was transparent again, of course. The maggots had gone. Had they ever been there? Did it matter? She began to laugh.

She was still laughing half-an-hour later when the sound of sirens filled the room and the ambulance arrived.

It wasn't fair.

Jeremy Martin lay in the bath thinking about the events of the past six weeks. It was hard not to think about them – in here, looking at the dents his daughter had made with the monkey-wrench. The taps had almost been beyond repair. As it was they now dripped all the time and the letter C was gone for ever. Old water, not Cold water.

He had seen Isabel a few days before and she had looked a lot better. She still wasn't talking but it would be a long time before that happened, they said. Nobody knew why she had decided to attack the bath – except maybe that fat friend of hers and she was too frightened to say. According to the experts, it had all been stress-related. A traumatic stress disorder. Of course they had fancy words for it. What they meant was that it was her parents who were to blame. They argued. There was tension in the house. Isabel hadn't been able to cope and had come up with some sort of fantasy related to the bath.

In other words, it was his fault.

But was it? As he lay in the soft, hot water with the smell of pine bath-oil rising up his nostrils, Jeremy Martin thought long and hard. He wasn't the one who started the arguments. It was always Susan. From the day he married her, she'd insisted on...well, changing him. She was always nagging him. It was like that nickname of his at school. Mouse. They never took him seriously. She never took him seriously. Well, he would show her.

Lying back with the steam all around him, Jeremy found himself floating away. It was a wonderful feeling. He would start with Susan. Then there were a couple of boys in his French class. And, of course, the headmaster.

He knew just what he would do. He had seen it that morning in a junk shop in Hampstead. Victorian, he would have said. Heavy, with a smooth wooden handle and a solid, razor-sharp head.

Yes. He would go out and buy it the following morning. It was just what he needed. A good Victorian axe...

Enter the strange and twisted
world of Anthony Horowitz –

if you dare!

ISBN 1 84121 364 0   £3.99

Two twisted tales to curdle your blood.

David's mobile won't stop ringing, but these are no ordinary callers. He seems to have a hotline to heaven...or hell.

Isabel has a nasty feeling that the Victorian bath her parents have installed is *waiting* for her. But it won't be a bubble bath she gets, more of a bloodbath.

ISBN 1 84121 366 7   £3.99

Two spine-chilling stories guaranteed to keep you awake at night.

Jamie is pleased with the camera he finds at a car boot sale, until he realises that everything he photographs breaks...or dies.

Henry soon finds that his new computer has a life of its own, and it's not afraid to gamble - with people's lives!

ISBN 1 84121 368 3   £3.99

Three
~~Two~~ **creepy stories to send shivers
down your spine.**

Uncle Nigel is determined to get a sun tan. But Tim is sure there's something sinister going on as his uncle's skin starts to frazzle and his brain begins to fry.

When Bart buys a magical monkey's ear in a market in Marrakesh, he discovers that making wishes is a dangerous game.

ISBN 1 84121 370 5   £3.99

Three sinister stories to fill you with fear.

Gary hates the countryside. It's boring. But something has got it in for Gary. Perhaps the countryside hates him too?

Kevin loves computer games, but this latest one breaks all the rules, and it's ruthless....

Howard's in heaven...so why does it feel more like hell?

ISBN 1 84121 372 1 £3.99

Three terrifying tales you'll wish you'd never read.

It's Halloween but the living dead on the night bus home aren't trick-or-treaters!

When his dad picks up a hitchhiker, Jacob finds himself in a life-or-death situation. Someone is harbouring a deadly secret.

And who is the man with the yellow face in Peter's passport photo – because it isn't him, is it?

ISBN 1 84121 374 8 £3.99

Two spooky stories guaranteed
to give you nightmares.

All the previous owners of Twist Cottage have died suddenly.
Surely a coincidence, thinks Ben. But is it?

Harriet is having a horrible dream, but any minute now she'll
wake up and it will all be OK...won't it?

More Orchard Black Apples

Orchard Black Apples are available from all good bookshops,
or can be ordered direct from the publisher:
Orchard Books, PO BOX 29, Douglas IM99 1BQ
Credit card orders please telephone 01624 836000
or fax 01624 837033
or e-mail: bookshop@enterprise.net for details.

To order please quote title, author and ISBN
and your full name and address.
Cheques and postal orders should be made payable to 'Bookpost plc.'
Postage and packing is FREE within the UK
(overseas customers should add £1.00 per book).

Prices and availability are subject to change.